The De Winton Foundry

Think of all the foundry men,
That worked the furnace everyday,
Those skilful workers, stoking fires,
Making moulds from sand and clay.
Smelting metal, glowing red.
"By Gum, it's hot!" the workers said.

So when you see the iron engines,
Steaming through, chuffing on,
Think of all the foundry people,
Their skills and labour now long gone.

Published in 2022 by
Saddletank Books

SADDLETANK BOOKS

Printed and bound
in Wales

ISBN
978-1-7397510-0-5

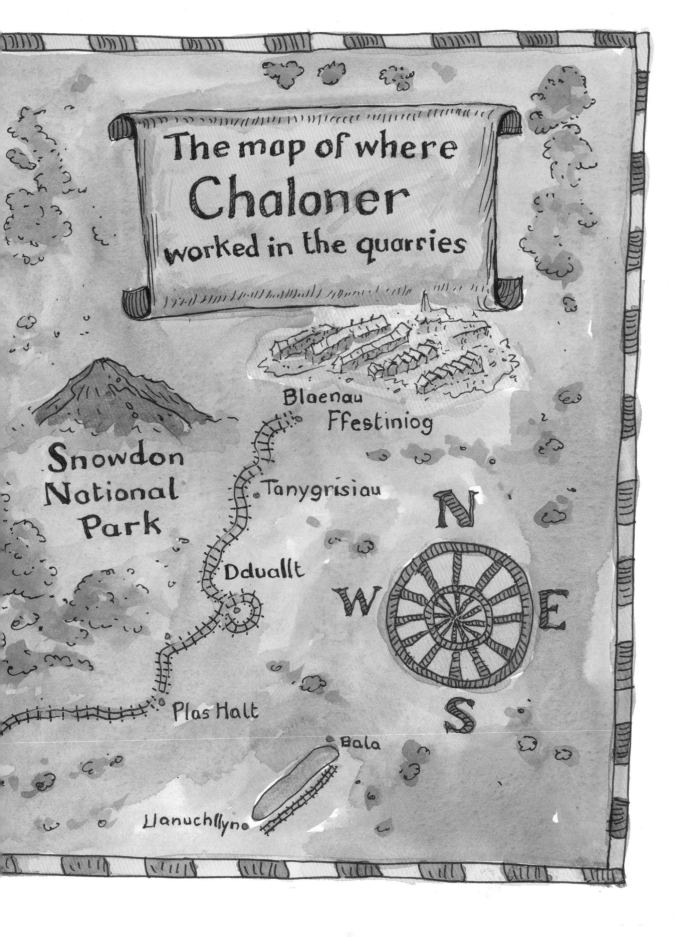

At the De Winton Foundry, they made steamships, girders, bridges boilers, winders, slate dressers, steam engines...and so much more!

Today another engine was leaving the workshop, Mr De Winton was there with his housekeeper to say goodbye.
"Look Ellen," he said, "this is Chaloner, our very first quarry engine with a cab."
"My goodness, he's grand," she said. "That'll keep the drivers warm and toasty."
"And I have a vertical boiler too." said Chaloner, proudly.

Then the little loco was hauled onto a wagon and off he went up the mountain, to the quarry.

The quarrymen loved Chaloner with his beautiful cab and tall chinmey. Another little coffee pot engine was already there and they both quickly set to work.

Chuff, chuff, chuffing, all day long they went, shunting wagons of slate.
Chaloner left a trail of embers behind him, as he didn't have an ash pan.

Each night his driver left a little fire in the grate and a lid on the chimney,
so that every morning his boiler would bubble away quickly.

Now as it happens, just when you least expect it, things can change.
There were over fifty quarries in the mountains and although everyone
worked very hard, after ten years, there was a lull, and this quarry
had to close!
"You can stay in the shed," said the quarry men.

"No point in feeling glum," said Chaloner, and he settled down for a rest.

Sure enough, only a few months later, there was an auction, and the two engines were sold to another larger quarry.
"Is it far away?" asked Chaloner.
"No," they said. " Just next door." And off they went.

At the new quarry, four more coffee pot engines were already there to greet them...and they all eyed Chaloner's cab.

" You're too tall to work in our tunnels," said the manager.
"That cab and chimney have to go!"
"Oh no!" exclaimed Chaloner.
 But off they came, and he was given a shorter chimney

Suddenly Chaloner felt lighter. He could hear the driver singing.
"No point in moping," he thought, as he chuffed on into the
mountain tunnel.

Where once worked many horses, the six coffee pots, now did the job.
They pulled far more wagons, did more work and strung across the
valley, carrying even more slate, were seven Blondins,
 (named after the marvellous Monsieur Blondin, the tight rope walker).

Chaloner's driver kept a little kettle
on his boiler, full of oil,
to lubricate the cylinders.
"Pour a bit more won't you,
so I don't seize up,"
said the little loco.

Now although Chaloner didn't slip like other engines, stopping could be difficult.

When he had a full load
in heavy rain,
his wooden brakes
wouldn't work well
on the wet rails...
and he would topple
off the slate tip...

...but the quarrymen always fixed him up.

Chaloner worked all day with his driver
and the young boy
who changed the points.
"Hurry up!" cried Chaloner.

So much slate was being quarried that three Hunslets, called Britomart, Sybil and Una, were ordered. They soon arrived. "We have cabs!" they said smirking.

All was ticking along quite nicely until... the new chairman arrived...

...Professor Otto Darbishire.
(an expert on botany)

He loved
lichens
far more
than
engines !

He would visit
the quarry...
frown at
the
four ton,
coffee pots

..and smile benignly at the
heavy, seven ton, Hunslets.

One day, he said, "Bigger is better,....YOU HAVE TO GO!"

Then he hopped onto his bike, and pedalled off
back to the university where he worked.

He was happily pondering lichens and didn't notice
a fast car career around the corner.
There was a terrible crash.

"Aaaagh!" cried the Prof, as
he fell off his bike.

He was quickly whisked off to hospital. A new manager had to be found.

...and so they did.
Along came
his cousin,
Mary Barnes

"Oh my goodness!" cried Mary when she was told about the Prof's plans.

'You certainly can not!!" she said. "RECYCLE AND REFURBISH!" she cried.

...and Chaloner was given a new boiler,
and they all carried on working.

Busy, busy busy,
all day long they went.

Rock from the tunnels to the winders,
rock from the winders to the mill,
waste from the mill to the tip,
slate from the mills to the Hunslets,
and off down the valley went the slate,
all day long.

Many years passed and
much slate was quarried.

But as time went by less slate was wanted and Mary came to see the engines. "I'm afraid it's time to close" she said

"Oh dear!" sighed Chaloner, as he was left abandoned in the mill .
'Stay strong," he mumbled to himself as more unwanted engines arrived.
"Change is good" he muttered. Then he started to chat to the other engines
...to cheer them up.

Now, Chaloner is just the right size to fit into a garden. Someone wanted him, of course!

One sunny day, the rusty, dusty little loco was pulled out of the mill, loaded onto a wagon and lowered slowly down the incline.

Off he went, far away from the quarries to his new home.

His new owner was delighted to see him arrive..
"Time to start cleaning you up," said Alf and patted his boiler.
"Thank you ", wheezed Chaloner.

People came to see the little engine.
"You know he can't stay here," said Alf's friend, the Rev Teddy.
"He needs a railway. He needs to be moving again!"

They set to;

cleaning,

de-rusting,

fixing his pipes

and lubricators,

replacing boiler bits

and other parts,

and painting...

...until finally he was all set to go...

Off he went to the
Leighton Buzzard Railway
to pull coaches of people. Everyone was
amazed to see a little coffee pot engine!

Chaloner was happy to be steaming again.
"Thank you," he said beaming.
"I like it here. Toot toot," he whistled as
he set off down the line.

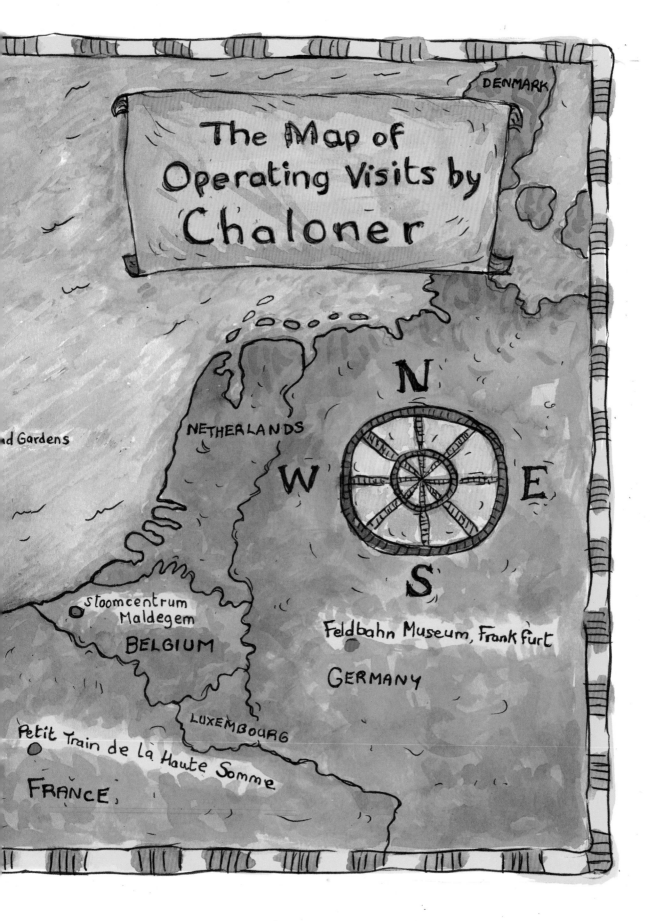

'The End'

If you have enjoyed this book maybe you'd like to read other books in the series or have a go at making one of the litttle engine models that go with the books. Remember, you can visit all the engines in the books because they're **real !!**

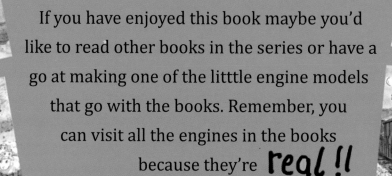

SADDLETANK BOOKS

and there's more info at
www.saddletankbooks.com

where to see the engines,... sketching tips,... loads of history facts,... events to visit, ...and the shop

Follow Saddletank Books on FB and Instagram too to see all the latest sketches and news